Chuck
and
Duck

Level 2B

Written by Sam Hay
Illustrated by Ann Johns
Reading Consultant: Betty Franchi

About Phonics

Spoken English uses more than 40 speech sounds. Each sound is called a *phoneme*. Some phonemes relate to a single letter (d-o-g) and others to combinations of letters (sh-ar-p). When a phoneme is written down, it is called a *grapheme*. Teaching these sounds, matching them to their written form, and sounding out words for reading is the basis of phonics.

Early phonics instruction gives children the tools to sound out, blend, and say the words without having to rely on memory or guesswork. This instruction gives children the confidence and ability to read unfamiliar words, helping them progress toward independent reading.

About the Consultant

Betty Franchi is an American educator with
a Bachelor's Degree in Elementary and Middle
Education as well as a Master's Degree in Special
Education. Betty holds a National Boards for
Professional Teaching Standards certification.
Throughout her 24 years as a teacher, she has
studied and developed an expertise in Phonetic
Awareness and has implemented phonetic strategies,
teaching many young children to read, including
students with special needs.

Reading tips

 This book focuses on the *ch* sound.

Tricky and/or new words in this book

Any words in bold may have unusual spellings or are new and have not yet been introduced.

Tricky and/or new words in this book

**said to for ball was
I my the friend**

Extra ways to have fun with this book

After the readers have finished the story, ask them questions about what they have just read.

What does Duck do well?
Why did Fred go red?

Explain that the two letters *ch* make one sound. Think of other words that use the *ch* sound, such as *chip* and *chat*.

I like to read and quack. My favorite place to read is in the park. Quack!

A Pronunciation Guide

This grid highlights the sounds used in the story and offers a guide on how to say them.

s	a	t	p	i
as in sat	as in ant	as in tin	as in pig	as in ink
n	c	e	h	r
as in net	as in cat	as in egg	as in hen	as in rat
m	d	g	o	u
as in mug	as in dog	as in get	as in ox	as in up
l	f	b	j	v
as in log	as in fan	as in bag	as in jug	as in van
w	z	y	k	qu
as in wet	as in zip	as in yet	as in kit	as in quick
x	ff	ll	ss	zz
as in box	as in off	as in ball	as in kiss	as in buzz
ck	pp	nn	rr	gg
as in duck	as in puppy	as in bunny	as in arrow	as in egg
dd	bb	tt	sh	ch
as in daddy	as in chubby	as in attic	as in shop	as in chip
th				
as in them				

Be careful not to add an /uh/ sound to /s/, /t/, /p/, /c/, /h/, /r/, /m/, /d/, /g/, /l/, /f/ and /b/. For example, say /ff/ not /fuh/ and /sss/ not /suh/.

Chuck got a shock.
A duck sat on his mat.

"Yes?" **said** Chuck.
"Quack!" said Duck.

Chuck went **to** chop a log.
Duck went as well.

Chuck went **for** a jog.
Duck went as well!

Chuck met his **friend** Fred
and his pet dog Chip.

Chuck and Fred had a chat.

"Duck is not a good pet," said Fred.

"Can Duck jump up for a **ball**?" said Fred.

"Not much," said Chuck.

"Can Duck run fast?"
said Fred.

"Not much," said Chuck.

"Duck is such a dull pet,"
said Fred.

Duck went off in a huff.

But Fred and Chuck got a shock.

Duck **was** back.
Duck had set up a game!

A rich man went past.
"**I** wish Duck was **my** pet.
How much?" said **the** man.

"Bad luck," said Chuck.
"Duck is my pet and best friend."
Fred went red!

OVER 48 TITLES IN SIX LEVELS
Betty Franchi recommends...

Some titles from Level 1

I love reading phonics **Bad Rat**

I love reading phonics **The Best Gift**

I love reading phonics **Clint and Grant Play I-Spy**

I love reading phonics **Bret and Grandma's Trip!**

978 1 84898 747 0   978 1 84898 750 0   978 1 84898 752 4   978 1 84898 751 7

Other titles to enjoy from Level 2

I love reading phonics **Wish Fish**

I love reading phonics **Let's go to the Swings**

I love reading phonics **Kyle in Trouble**

978 1 84898 755 5   978 1 84898 759 3   978 1 84898 762 3

Some titles from Level 3

I love reading phonics **Bart's Go-Cart**

I love reading phonics **Queen Ella's Feet**

I love reading phonics **Puff Flies**

I love reading phonics **The Pop Duet**

978 1 84898 768 5   978 1 84898 764 7   978 1 84898 765 4   978 1 84898 767 8

An Hachette Company
First Published in the United States by TickTock, an imprint of Octopus Publishing Group.
www.octopusbooksusa.com

Copyright © Octopus Publishing Group Ltd 2013

Distributed in the US by
Hachette Book Group USA
237 Park Avenue, New York NY 10017, USA

Distributed in Canada by
Canadian Manda Group
165 Dufferin Street, Toronto, Ontario, Canada M6K 3H6

ISBN 978 1 84898 756 2

Printed and bound in China
10 9 8 7 6 5 4 3 2